1,2,3 suddenly in MEXICO

The Protective Jaguar

Cristina Falcón Maldonado

Illustrations: Marta Fàbrega

BARRON'S

On Martin's eighth birthday, his grandfather gave him a tiny package and said, "I've been an explorer all my life, and now it's your turn to see the world. Here is the key to my secret storeroom, where you'll find everything you'll need."

In the secret storeroom, Martin found maps and equipment as well as his grandfather's travel album and a strange necklace that came with these instructions:

ATTACH STOREROOM KEY TO NECKLACE. PUT NECKLACE ON.

CLOSE EYES. NAME DESIRED DESTINATION OUT LOUD.

"Amazing! I can travel anywhere!" Martin said. So that very day he
went to China. He explored the country and brought back a small pet dragon named See-me.
"What an adventure!" he thought. "Now where in the world should I go next?"

"Wow!" Martin said, sitting up in bed one morning. "I just had the strangest dream, and so real!"

See-me, his pet dragon, awakened immediately and wanted to hear about it.

"I was walking around a strange city with a jaguar," Martin said. "It was leading me somewhere."

Martin jumped out of bed and got dressed. "Let's go to the zoo," he said. "Maybe the jaguar there will give us a clue about my dream."

As soon as Martin and See-me got near the jaguar's enclosure, the big cat walked toward them, keeping his eyes on Martin.

"He's trying to tell me something," Martin whispered, "I know. But what? I am going to check my grandfather's travel album."

4-5

Martin opened the album and soon learned that most of the ancient peoples in Mexico had a jaguar god. "Jaguars were symbols of power and strength," he read. "They protected the rulers."

Martin got out his backpack and began filling it with everything that he'd need for a trip. "I'm sure that my dream and the jaguar in the zoo were telling me that it's time for our next adventure," he said. He put on the magic necklace, picked up See-me with one hand and his backpack with the other. He closed his eyes and said, "MEXICO!" Then one, two, three, suddenly . . .

6-7

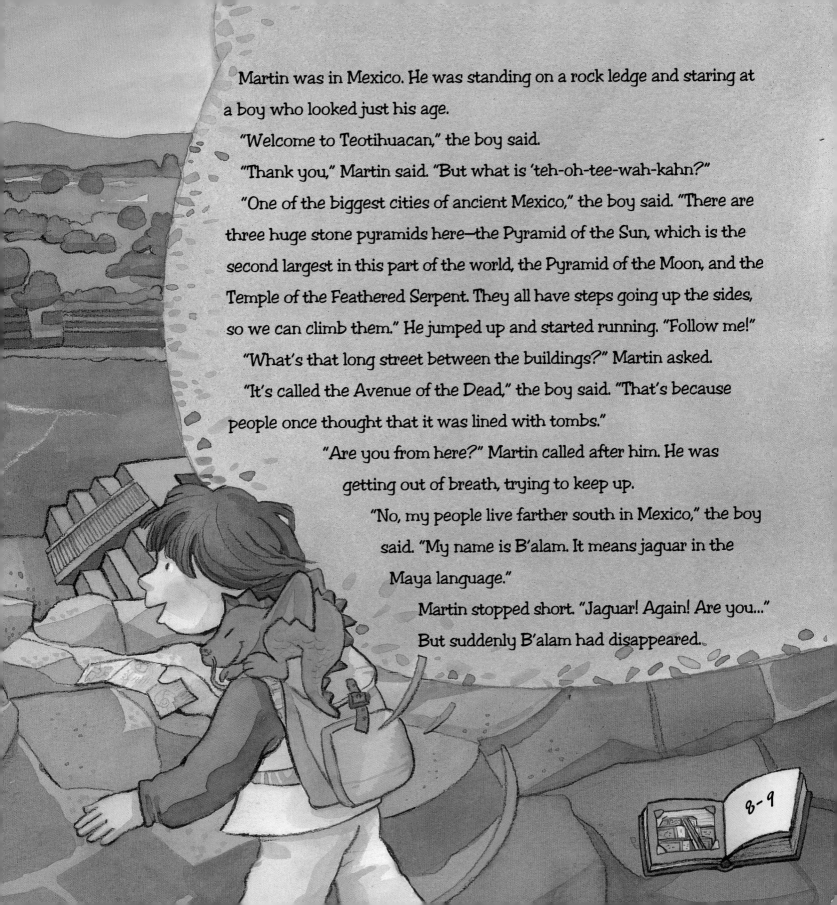

Martin was in Mexico. He was standing on a rock ledge and staring at a boy who looked just his age.

"Welcome to Teotihuacan," the boy said.

"Thank you," Martin said. "But what is 'teh-oh-tee-wah-kahn?'"

"One of the biggest cities of ancient Mexico," the boy said. "There are three huge stone pyramids here—the Pyramid of the Sun, which is the second largest in this part of the world, the Pyramid of the Moon, and the Temple of the Feathered Serpent. They all have steps going up the sides, so we can climb them." He jumped up and started running. "Follow me!"

"What's that long street between the buildings?" Martin asked.

"It's called the Avenue of the Dead," the boy said. "That's because people once thought that it was lined with tombs."

"Are you from here?" Martin called after him. He was getting out of breath, trying to keep up.

"No, my people live farther south in Mexico," the boy said. "My name is B'alam. It means jaguar in the Maya language."

Martin stopped short. "Jaguar! Again! Are you..."

But suddenly B'alam had disappeared.

8-9

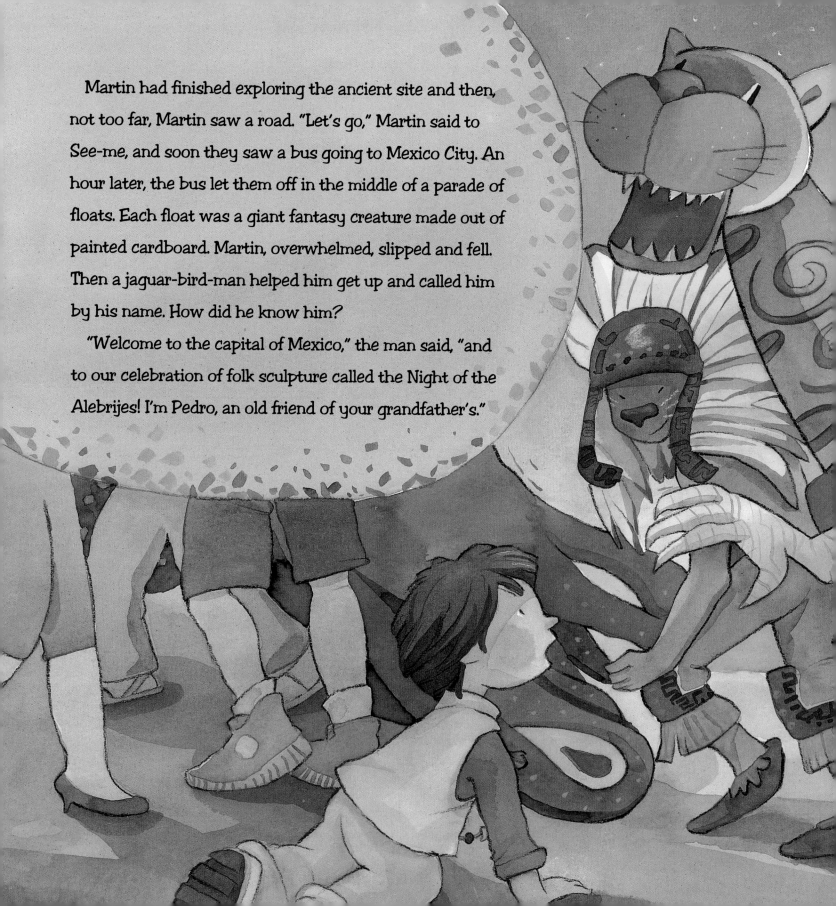

Martin had finished exploring the ancient site and then, not too far, Martin saw a road. "Let's go," Martin said to See-me, and soon they saw a bus going to Mexico City. An hour later, the bus let them off in the middle of a parade of floats. Each float was a giant fantasy creature made out of painted cardboard. Martin, overwhelmed, slipped and fell. Then a jaguar-bird-man helped him get up and called him by his name. How did he know him?

"Welcome to the capital of Mexico," the man said, "and to our celebration of folk sculpture called the Night of the Alebrijes! I'm Pedro, an old friend of your grandfather's."

When the parade ended, Pedro said, "You must be even hungrier than I am. We'll go to the local *taquería*—the best taco shop in town."

Pedro's wife, Lupe, and his son, Diego, were waiting at the shop.

"We'll celebrate your arrival with a Mexican feast," Lupe said.

While Martin was trying the tacos, enchiladas, and quesadillas, he noticed that See-me was chewing a hot pepper.

"*Oye!*" Diego shouted. "Your dragon is breathing fire!"

12-13

The next day, Martin's new friends took him to the *Zócalo*. "This public square has been the center of two cities," Lupe said. "The first was the capital of the great Aztec empire, created almost seven hundred years ago."

"Didn't the Spanish conquer the Aztecs?" Martin asked.

"Yes, they destroyed the Aztec capital and built Mexico City on the ruins," Pedro said. "They constructed the Metropolitan Cathedral and National Palace right here. The remains of the Aztec *Templo Mayor*, or Great Temple, are just a few steps away."

Diego took Martin inside the National Palace to see the murals that illustrated Mexico's history. "Another Diego painted these," he said. "Diego Rivera, one of our most famous artists."

14-15

Their next stop was the National Museum of Anthropology.

"That's *la Piedra del Sol*—the Sun Stone," Diego said, pointing to an enormous disc. "The Aztecs carved symbols on it that tell the history of the universe and the destruction of four worlds. The sun god is in the center."

"It must weigh a ton," Martin said.

"Twenty-four tons, actually!" Diego said. He motioned Martin to follow him. "Let's look at the exhibits about the Maya, Olmec, and other ancient peoples."

16-17

That afternoon Lupe took Martin and See-me to the canals of Xochimilco.

"It looks like people are having a party on every one of these boats," Martin said.

Lupe nodded. "The boats are *trajineras*. A ride on the canals with food and music is a popular outing for Mexicans and tourists. During the time of the Aztecs there was a large lake here, and much of the food for the capital was grown on it."

"How do you grow food on a lake?" Martin asked.

"The farmers created small islands called *chinampas* out of mud and planted their crops on them," Lupe explained. "Today some *chinampas* remain still, and farmers grow flowers as well as vegetables on them."

Martin noticed that See-me was about to join one of the parties. "Hey, wait for us!" Martin shouted.

"This is my first rodeo ever," Martin said on the morning they arrived in Guadalajara, Mexico's second largest city.

"Viva la charreada!" Diego cheered. "The rodeo is our national sport!"

"The *charreada* has ten events to test the skills of riders," Pedro said as they took their seats, "and we're lucky enough to watch them all in the oldest *lienzo,* or arena, in Mexico."

"Look at that *charro* ride!" Martin shouted. "He's stayed on the bronco far longer than any of the other cowboys."

"I wish I could ride like that," said Diego with a wishful look.

20-21

Martin and his friends made a detour on the way back to Mexico City to see two famous volcanoes, Iztaccihuatl and Popocatepetl.

"We call them Izta and Popo," Diego said, "and there's a legend about them. Will you tell it, Dad?"

"Sure," Pedro said. "Long ago a princess named Izta fell in love with Popo, one of her father's warriors. Izta's father disliked Popo and sent him off to war in a faraway place. Then he told Izta that her beloved had been killed in battle. Izta died of grief. But Popo returned. When he discovered that Izta was dead, he carried her here and laid her down on the ground. Filled with rage, he knelt beside her. The gods turned them both into snow-covered volcanoes. Izta lies quietly now. But Popo still erupts with fury, sending fire and rocks raining down on the land."

"Get up, Martin!" Diego said early one morning. "It's *el Dia de los Muertos*—the Day of the Dead. We've got a lot to prepare for the celebration."

"Celebration?" Martin asked. "It doesn't sound very happy."

"But it is!" Diego said. "All the relatives get together. We pray for our loved ones who've died. We make a special altar called an *ofrenda*, put flowers and their favorite foods on it, and take it to the cemetery."

"It's a way of honoring the dead," Lupe said, "but also a way of keeping the whole family close together."

"That's one of my favorite things about the holiday," Diego said. "I get to see all my cousins."

Diego and Martin went to the market to buy the traditional *calaveritas de dulce*."

"Sugar skulls!" Martin shouted. "What a combination! They're both sweet and creepy."

The next day, Martin and his friends traveled to Monte Albán in southern Mexico to visit the ancient capital of the Zapotec people.

"We don't know the Zapotec name for this mountaintop city," Lupe said, "but we do know that their empire was strong for a thousand years."

Martin toured the vast site. There were pyramids, temples, public squares, and even a ball court. At the bottom of one pyramid, he wandered into a passageway to look at the animal carvings. After a few minutes, he realized that he was lost. His heart began to pound, and he was starting to panic when he noticed the image of a jaguar. Martin hurried toward it and saw a shaft of light. The exit!

"Help from a jaguar...again!" Martin said to himself.

26-27

The next stop was a tropical forest in the state of Chiapas. Two of Diego's cousins joined them for a hike. No sooner had they set out than a deafening noise seemed to shake the jungle.

"What is that?" Martin shouted.

"A howler monkey," Pedro shouted back. "Some say it is the loudest land animal on Earth—and I believe it!"

Martin turned to get away from the noise and saw an ancient temple that rose high into the sky.

"That's where we're headed—to the ruins of Palenque," Lupe said. "Get ready to meet one of the most interesting peoples of the ancient world—the Maya."

When Martin and his friends reached Palenque's *Templo de las Inscripciones*, or Temple of Inscriptions, a magnificent green and red bird swooped down.

"A quetzal!" Pedro said. "The Maya kings used this bird's long tail feathers as a sign of authority. One king, Pakal the Great, ruled Palenque for sixty-eight years and made it a great city. His tomb is in this temple. It was finished by his son, Kan B'alam II."

"I've met someone called B'alam," Martin said. "The name means jaguar."

When they entered the temple, they saw large tablets covered with hieroglyphs—writing that uses small pictures for words and sounds.

"The Maya were the only ancient people in the Americas to have a complete writing system," Diego said. "They were also fine mathematicians and astronomers. They even measured how long it takes the Earth to revolve around the sun, and their numbers were extremely accurate."

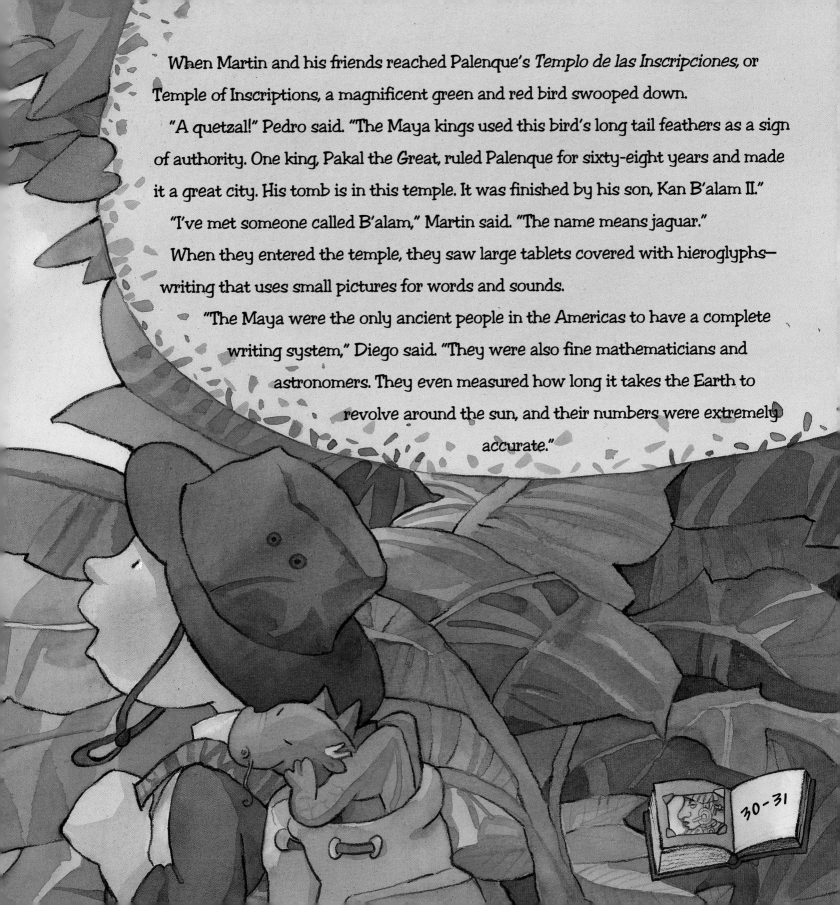

30-31

The travelers spent Diego's birthday in Cancún, a popular place to vacation on the Caribbean Sea.

"Hurray!" Diego shouted. "The *piñata* has been hung!"

He took the first turn trying to hit the clay *piñata* with a stick while blindfolded. His cousin Marina gave the *piñata* an even harder *thwack!* At once, candy came raining down on all of them!

Before Martin's friends returned home, they explored the Maya city of Chichen Itza with him. They saw the ancient steam baths, the stone rings that were used in ball games, and the Pyramid of Kukulcan, where the shadow of Quetzalcoatl, the feathered serpent god, slithers down its steps on some days of the year.

"I've had a great time seeing Mexico with you," Martin said. "Thank you for everything!" Standing next to the serpent's head at the bottom of the pyramid, Martin embraced them and waved till they were gone. Suddenly, someone tapped him on the shoulder. He spun around.

"B'alam!" Martin said, staring at the boy whom he'd met on his first day in Mexico. "You keep appearing and disappearing!"

B'alam grinned. "I've come to give you this charm. It's made of obsidian, a volcanic glass that my ancestors used for tools and in religious ceremonies. It will protect you on your way home."

B'alam waved—and then he was gone.

Martin put on the magic necklace and called to See-me. Once the dragon was safely in his arms, Martin closed his eyes and said, "HOME!"

34-35

1,2,3 suddenly in
MEXICO
The Protective Jaguar

GLOSSARY

TEMPLE OF THE FEATHERED SERPENT: A pyramid dedicated to Quetzalcoatl, god of water and wind and master creator of the universe for the ancient people of Mexico. It is represented by the figure of a bird-snake, decorated with quetzal feathers. (Page 9)

ALEBRIJE: Fantasy creature, appearing in dreams, combining the characteristics of several animals in a single figure. (Page 10)

TACOS, ENCHILADAS, AND QUESADILLAS: Traditional Mexican food, quick to prepare and very popular, made from corn or wheat tortillas folded in half, rolled up or fried and filled with meat, cheese, beans, vegetables, and sauces. (Page 13)

ZÓCALO: The most important public place in the city, its monumental center and main square. (page 15)

TRAJINERA: A large canoe, typical of Xochimilco, used to take visitors on trips along the canals. Each boat has its name painted on it. (Page 19)

CHINAMPAS: A floating plot of land or garden, invented by the first inhabitants of Mexico, on which flowers and vegetables are grown. (Page 19)

CHARRO: Mexican horse rider, skilled in the use of a whip and breaking in horses, wearing a suit with a short jacket and bordered trousers, a white shirt, and a hat with a broad rim and high crown. (Page 21)

QUETZAL: One of the most beautiful birds in the world, with iridescent green feathers and a very long brightly colored tail. It lives in the rain forests of Mexico and Guatemala. (Page 31)

First edition for the United States and Canada published in 2011 by Barron's Educational Series, Inc.
© Copyright 2010 by Gemser Publications, S.L.
C/Castell, 38; Teià (08329) Barcelona, Spain (World Rights)
Author: Cristina Falcón Maldonado
Adaptation of English text: Joanne Barkan
Illustrator: Marta Fàbrega

All inquiries should be addressed to:
Barron's Educational Series, Inc.
250 Wireless Boulevard
Hauppauge, NY 11788
www.barronseduc.com

ISBN-13: 978-0-7641-4585-8
ISBN-10: 0-7641-4585-1
Library of Congress Control Number: 2010931208

Date of Manufacture: December 2010
Manufactured by: L. Rex Printing, Tin Wan, Aberdeen, Hong Kong

Printed in China
9 8 7 6 5 4 3 2 1